HPL HPY EBH
HOW CLC

The

The

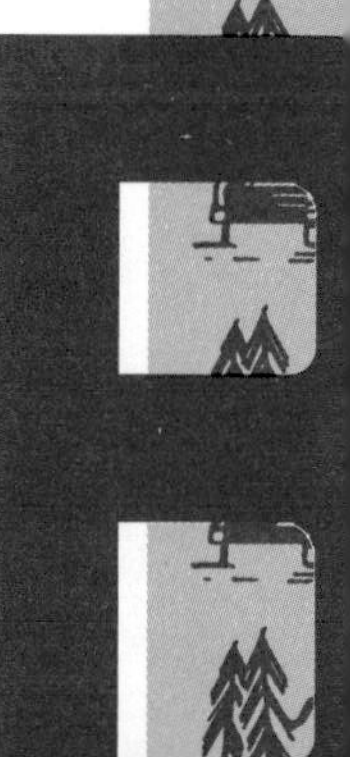

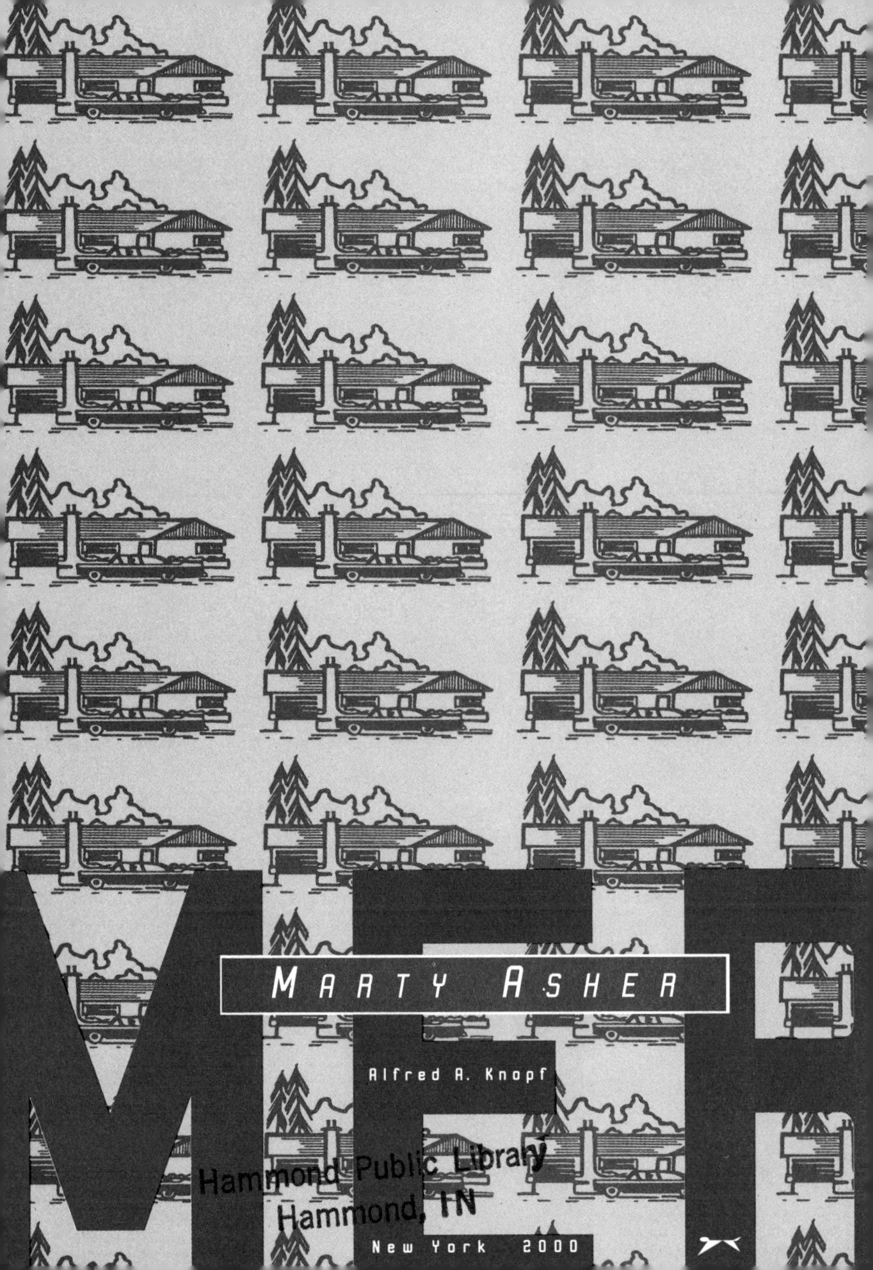
MARTY ASHER
Alfred A. Knopf
Hammond Public Library
Hammond, IN
New York 2000

THIS IS A BORZOI BOOK

PUBLISHED BY ALFRED A. KNOPF

 Published in the United States by Alfred A. Knopf, a division of Random House, Inc., New York, and simultaneously in Canada by Random House of Canada Limited, Toronto. Distributed by Random House, Inc., New York.

www.aaknopf.com

Knopf, Borzoi Books, and the colophon are registered trademarks of Random House, Inc.

Library of Congress Cataloging-in-Publication Data
Asher, Marty.
The boomer / by Marty Asher. — 1st ed.
p. cm.
ISBN 0-375-41009-0
I. Title.
PS3551.S375 B66 2000
813'.54 99-049238
CIP

Manufactured in the United States of America

First Edition

DESIGNED BY CHIP KIDD

THE B MER

boom•er (bü′mər), *n.* 1: a person or thing that booms. 2: a person who settles in areas or towns that are booming. 3: *informal:* BABY BOOMER

1.

The boomer was born on a Friday. He weighed six pounds, eight ounces. He was named after his grandfather, who had re-arranged the family name to make it sound more American. The boomer's mother said he was a happy baby who never cried. As a toddler, his favorite activities were painting, reading and banging pots with spoons.

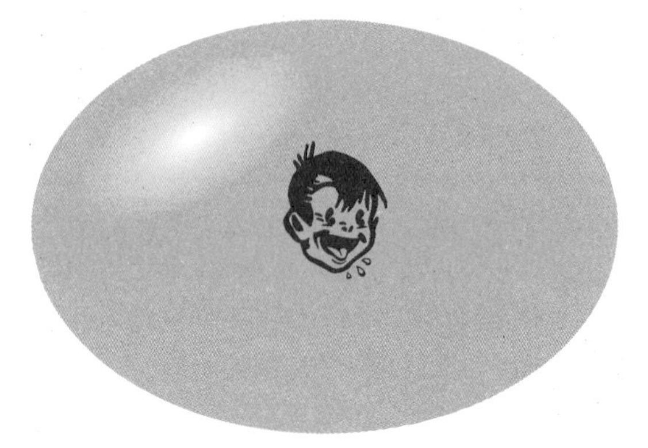

2.

The boomer's favorite lunch was a fried egg. He liked to stab the yolk with his fork and watch it spawn little rivers, in which he would float bits of bread off to war.

3.

The boomer and his family went to the country on a summer vacation. One morning he saw a drowned mouse at the edge of the lake. The boomer and his friend extracted it with a shovel, covered the body with an O'Henry bar wrapper and buried the mouse on a nearby hill. They marked the grave with a cross made out of twigs and a rubber band. The boomer didn't know exactly what the cross meant, but it felt serious.

4.

Once the boomer stole some money from a charity can that his parents kept on top of a cabinet. He also stole quarters from his mother's purse. When she discovered the theft, his mother screamed at him. He wondered if he would go to hell. It felt exciting.

5.

His parents lived on the third floor of a small walk-up tenement. The boomer's favorite place to play was in a corner of the kitchen under a stepladder, which, he decided, would protect him if a hydrogen bomb fell.

6.

The boomer also liked to play in the bathroom. He cut newspapers into strips and pretended they were secret messages. After soaking them in water, he wrapped the strips around the top of a hot radiator pipe that ran from ceiling to floor. When the strips dried, they slid down the pipe to the army.

7.

Once the boomer was playing in the bathroom with his father's razor and nearly sliced off his thumb. It didn't hurt a lot, but he was surprised by the thickness and darkness of his blood. For the rest of his life he had a small crescent-shaped scar on the back of his thumb.

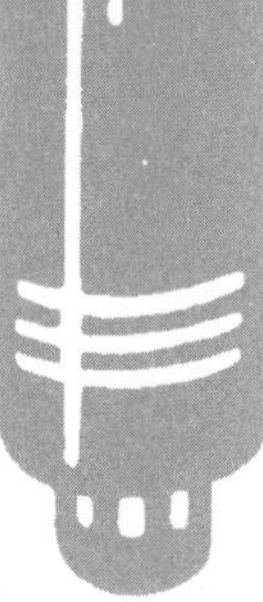

The boomer's father took him to school. It was raining. His father walked fast and dragged him through puddles. The boomer was a muddy mess when he arrived, but from the first day he loved school.

9.

The boomer almost always got excellent grades. When he failed a math test, his mother came to class to talk to the teacher. The boomer felt ashamed to have everyone see his mother's frumpy green dress.

10.

School was predictable. When a teacher yelled at you, they were almost always right. Sometimes his mother hit him for no reason at all.

11.

The boomer stole a comic book from a mailbox in the hallway. That night he read it under his covers with a flashlight. Then he tore it into little pieces and flushed it down the toilet.

12.

The boomer had three best friends. His first best friend lived in his building. They played ball together and made jokes about women's tits. When the boomer went to the beach with his friend, they would stop older pretty girls and say that the other one wanted a kiss but was too shy to ask. Sometimes they would get a kiss, or even money. Sometimes the girl's boyfriend would tell them to fuck off.

13.

The boomer's second best friend liked to draw with him. They created a comic strip about Sparky, a talking firefly who saved people in difficult situations. Sparky also rescued trapped animals.

14.

He got the idea for Sparky from a dream. The boomer had just robbed a store and was trapped against a garage wall, about to be captured by the police. Suddenly the wall opened and he was in a kind of boys' club where a man who looked like the man who played Tarzan took care of boys who were orphans. They had rooms where the walls went only halfway up so you could have some privacy but wouldn't feel too lonely.

15.

The boomer liked reading. For a while he thought love, war and death happened only in books. He especially liked science fiction.

16.

The boomer looked forward to his father's coming home from work so he could read the movie pages. When he grabbed the paper without saying hello, his father said sarcastically, "The newspaper is home."

17.

The children would send each other letters in school. Most of the letters said, "Will you please come to my birthday party?" The boomer usually received two or three letters, which was pretty good for a boy.

18.

The boomer wrote a really long letter. He asked the most popular girl to go to the movies with him. He told her the name of the movie, where it was playing, who it starred, the names of the producer and director, and the time schedule. The teacher was standing next to him as he wrote the letter. She smiled when she looked at it.

19.

In the sixth grade the boomer ran for school treasurer. On the day of the election he had a fever and had to stay home. At four o'clock the vice presidential candidate shouted up from the street, "You won." The boomer wondered if he could be President someday.

V

20.

The boomer liked watching television. He wished that funny things would happen in his family and that they would all hug at the end.

21.

A friend of his parents' was dying. They whispered, "He's very sick" and "Maybe there'll be a miracle," when they thought no one was listening. The boomer liked the man and prayed for him. When he died, it confirmed his worst suspicions about the world.

22.

In the boomer's favorite sexual fantasy, he was a wounded marine all bandaged up in a hospital where a beautiful nurse would draw the curtains around his bed and ask if there was anything she could do to ease his pain. He would tell her and she would do it.

23.

The boomer went to the senior prom with a tall girl. He pretended that he was drunk and having a good time. Later, they made out in her basement. When she asked him to stop, he was relieved.

24.

The boomer got strong college recommendations. He won a scholarship to a university on the other side of the country. His parents were proud, but sad that he was going so far away.

25.

The boomer was popular in college. He was a little shy, which made him nonthreatening to the boys and attractive to the girls. He hung out with the coolest kids. He learned about drugs.

26.

In college, the boomer had sex for the first time. Afterward the girl told him she was married but her husband, who was a student, wouldn't mind. When he saw her again, she introduced them. Her husband seemed like a really nice guy, though he looked a little sad. The boomer felt bad for him, but he was also impressed with himself.

27.

Having sex was the most fun the boomer had had since banging pots. Pursuing it became his preoccupation. He hoped someday he would fall in love, if love really existed; but in the meantime, sex would do just fine.

28.

The boomer took LSD. He had a vision that he ought to act more like Jesus, but when he came down he couldn't figure out how to do it. Music, colors and food were great too.

29.

The boomer's third best friend was his college roommate. They drank a lot, stayed up all night, and talked about love, the meaning of life, and becoming rich. One time they got stoned and ended up laughing in a tub full of bubble bath at four a.m. The boomer lost touch with his third best friend when he married a woman the boomer's wife hated.

30.

The boomer graduated with honors. He got a good job in a large company. He rented a small walk-up apartment. A woman gave him a cat.

31.

The cat was white with brown spots. It kept the boomer up nights purring on his pillow. The cat lived with him for eight years before it got run over by a school bus after the boomer and his family moved to the suburbs.

32.

The boomer had a party for the people in his office. He cooked chili from a recipe he had cut off the back of a rice box. Everyone got drunk and had a good time. The boomer felt he was like some of the people on television.

33.

Although he had many friends at work, the boomer sometimes felt lonely. He walked around the city so he could come home tired, play with the cat and go to sleep without thinking. Sometimes he had a glass or two of Scotch to help.

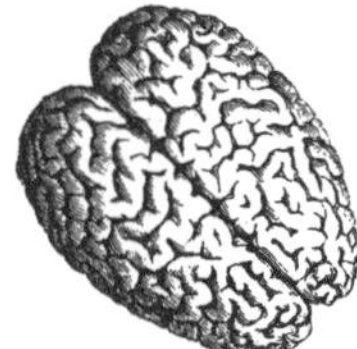

34.

The boomer's first therapist told him it was not unusual to feel lonely when starting out in life. He said he could relate to the boomer's pain because he had just gone through a divorce. He asked the boomer if he liked tennis. They played a few games together. While the boomer liked his therapist, he wasn't sure he wanted him as a tennis partner.

35.

The boomer bought a stereo. He collected 219 CDs in his lifetime. His favorites were Miles Davis (10 CDs), The Rolling Stones (7), Bob Dylan (5), Beethoven (4), John Coltrane, Bach, Fleetwood Mac, and Marvin Gaye (3).

36.

The boomer started to think about having a family of his own, like most of his friends were doing. Maybe his family would be happier than the one he grew up in.

37.

The boomer got along well with his superiors, co-workers and clients. He concentrated on priorities. He was quickly promoted.

38.

The boomer moved in with the woman who gave him the cat. He wasn't sure if he was in love, but being with her felt easy and natural.

39.

The boomer enjoyed having sex with one person. You didn't have to be nervous about your performance or what they would find offensive. He liked walking around the house naked and having breakfast with his girlfriend. She made great coffee.

40.

Regular sex took the edge off the boomer. It made him feel like a desirable adult demographic. He focused more on his career. He was promoted again.

41.

The boomer and his girlfriend got married. It was an outdoor ceremony. The boomer's wife wore a white antique cotton dress. The boomer wore an off-white linen suit. Everyone said it was a beautiful wedding.

42.

They went to a tropical island for their honeymoon. The boomer enjoyed sipping pink fruity cocktails with his wife on their terrace overlooking the ocean. One day they made love six times.

43.

Two weeks after the wedding, the boomer's father died suddenly. Six months later, his mother was killed in a hit-and-run accident. The people in the boomer's office sent large baskets of fruits and nuts.

44.

The boomer moved into a new apartment with his wife and the cat. They bought more furniture and things for the kitchen. Sometimes they made love before they did the dishes.

45.

When he left the hospital the morning his son was born, the boomer felt blinded by the bright sun outside. It was the happiest day of his life.

46.

The boomer stared at the miracle of his son's tiny but perfect body for two days before he went back to work. People from the office gave him a blue handmade patch quilt. He learned how to change the baby. He decided that he loved his wife.

47.

The boomer's son was a precocious, healthy baby who rarely cried. His favorite foods were spaghetti and Cheerios, preferably together. He strung them into necklaces before he ate them.

48.

One of the boomer's co-workers said, "It's never too early to start saving for college," and gave him his broker's card. It sounded silly and stuffy at the time, but calling the broker turned out to be one of the smartest things the boomer ever did.

49.

When the boomer's son talked, the boomer couldn't believe it. When he walked, that was amazing too. But after a while, being a parent became a little repetitive, like work, though there were still some really neat parts.

50.

It took the boomer a while to get used to saying "my wife" and "my son," because they didn't feel like "his" anything. He felt bad for people who didn't have wives and sons, because it must make them feel lonely to hear how full his life sounded, even if it didn't feel that way to him.

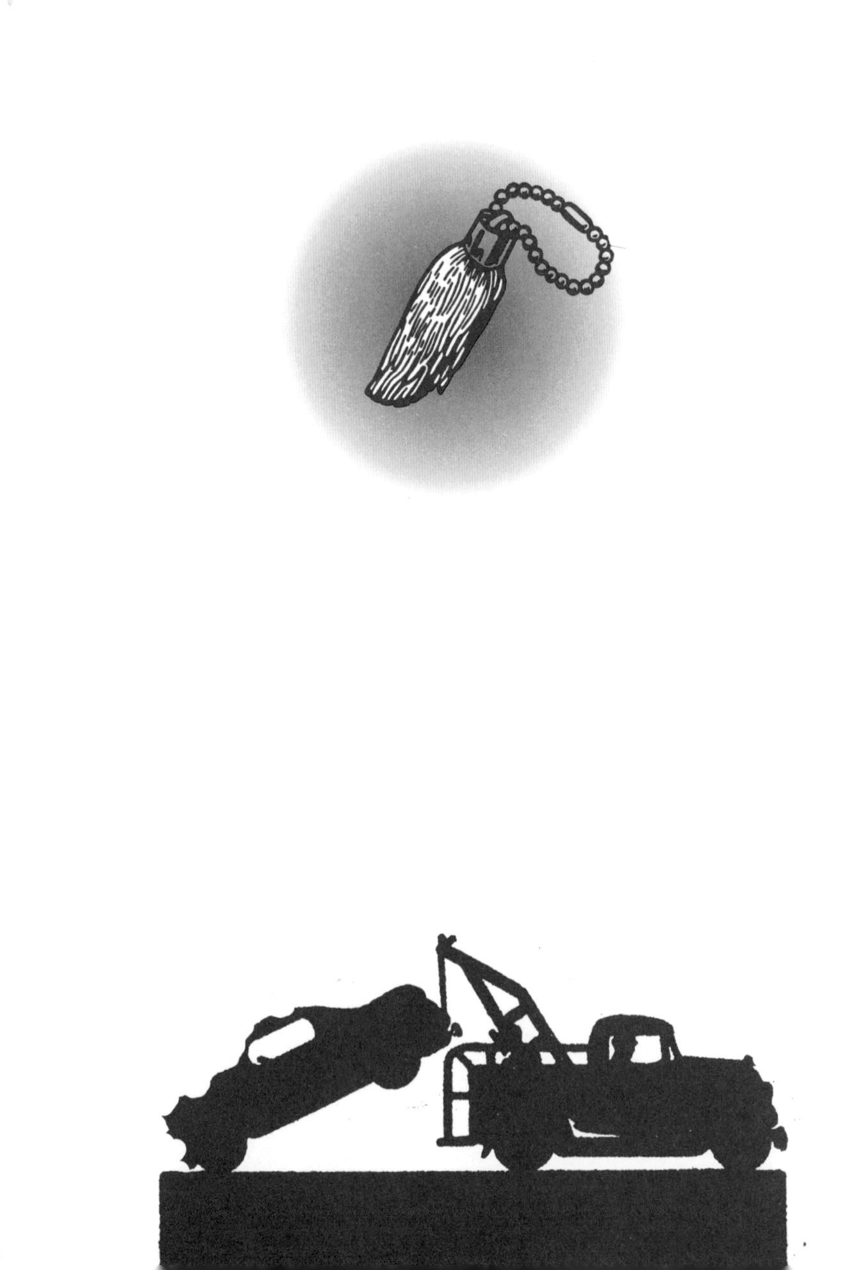

51.

The boomer's first car was a blue Toyota with 45,000 miles on it. After two years he totaled it in a head-on collision. No one was injured, but sometimes the boomer's son would wake up crying and ask, "What ever happened to the blue car?"

52.

The boomer invested regularly in the stock market. His stocks went up. His broker said that if anything happened to him, his investments would provide for his wife and son. This made the boomer feel both prudent and unnecessary.

LIBERTY
1985
LIBERTY
1985

53.

The boomer and his wife bought a house in the suburbs. The boomer's wife said the schools were good and they could use the outdoor space. Once they had a birthday party outside with umbrellas and balloons.

54.

The boomer's wife furnished the house. Their friends said it was cozy and elegant without being pretentious.

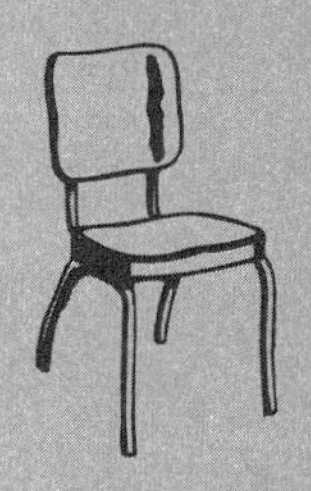

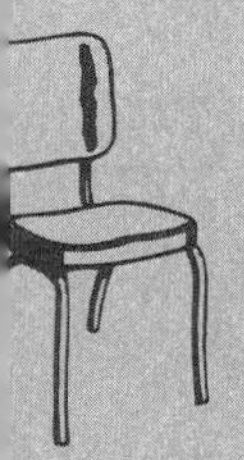

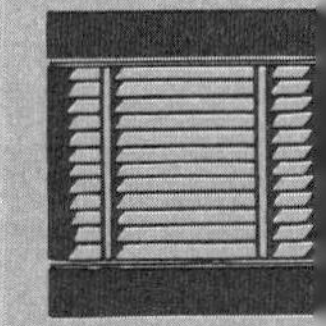

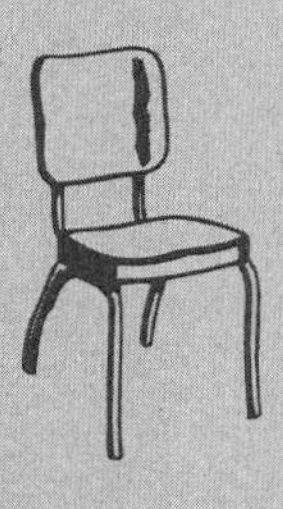

55.

The boomer's wife bought a brown hand-painted Chinese vase with a green-and-orange Buddha on it. The Buddha had large, nasty-looking eyebrows and wore a blue kerchief with gold spots. His head was surrounded by a white halo. The boomer put it on the top shelf of a bookcase between *The Stranger* and *Catch-22*.

56.

The boomer loved his son but found it hard to talk to him unless it was about something specific like solving an algebra problem or fixing the brakes on his bicycle. When he tried to hug him, it felt stiff and unnatural.

57.

The boomer's son insisted on getting a dog. After a week, he decided he didn't want it anymore because it drooled all over and stank up his room. The boomer said it was his responsibility. His son said no one forced him to get the dog.

58.

At night, when he walked the dog, the boomer would see his neighbors staring at their television screens. Sometimes they would turn and wave to him.

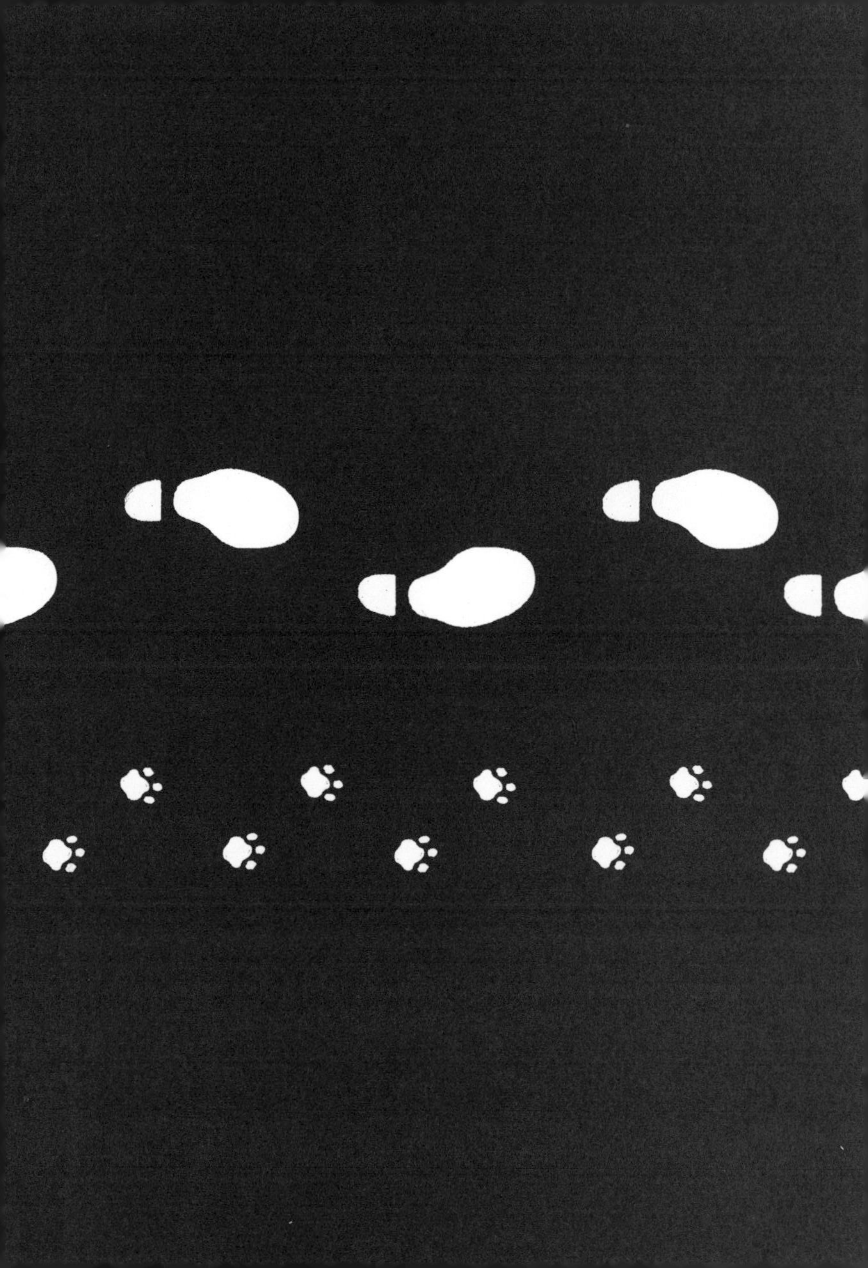

59.

The dog became his favorite member of the family. The happiest moment of the boomer's day was when the dog jumped up to the foot of the bed at night, sighed deeply, and started to snore.

60.

The boomer's wife said he should talk to his son about sex. They went for a walk on the beach. His son skipped stones. When he finished explaining everything he asked his son if he wanted to know anything else. "Can we have pizza for dinner?"

61.

The boomer took a multivitamin every day and an aspirin every other day. He watched his fat intake. He did not drink excessively except at an occasional party or if he was really depressed. When he couldn't sleep, he took Valium.

62.

The Valium was prescribed by the boomer's second psychiatrist. The boomer saw him when he started having problems sleeping because the quiet at night in the suburbs spooked him. The psychiatrist said the drug might take the edge off things until the boomer adjusted to his new surroundings. He also said exercise might help. He did not ask him to play tennis.

63.

The boomer bought a treadmill. He lost five pounds. He watched a lot of public television. He got two canvas bags, a mug and a set of meditation tapes.

64.

The boomer's wife loved him with an unshakable devotion and loyalty. It enraged him.

HUSBANDS
LOVE
WIVES
I LOVE
YOU

65.

Sometimes the boomer and his wife would make love three or four nights in a row, but then weeks could go by. Sex gradually changed from something wild and powerful to a more enjoyable version of a fun every-day activity, like taking a hot shower. The boomer also masturbated. He thought about the nurse.

66.

The boomer cheated on his wife three times. The first time was with a woman he met at a sales convention. The second was with the mother of one of his son's friends, who had just gotten divorced and was feeling lonely. The third was with a man who picked him up in a bar on a business trip.

2.

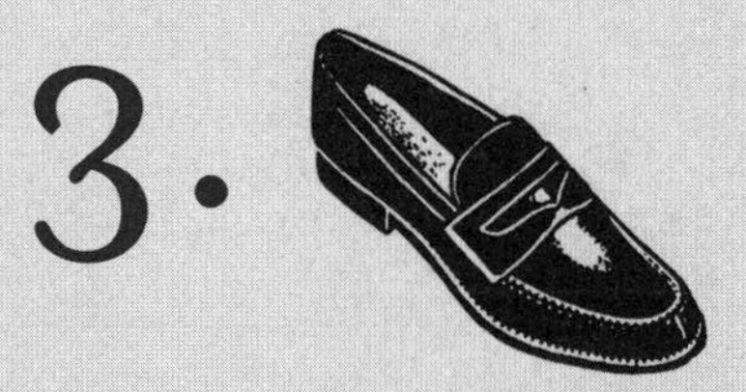

67.

Sex with a man was exciting but it left the boomer feeling lonely and confused. It wasn't something he would want to do regularly.

68.

A few of the boomer's friends got divorced. Some of them remarried. The boomer didn't think he would ever get divorced, but he worried that maybe his friends had felt the same way.

69.

The boomer's second car was a white Volvo station wagon. His son, who was twelve, called it a refrigerator on wheels. His son's lover totaled the Volvo when they were at college. By then the boomer had moved on to his third car, a red Saab convertible.

70.

He was courted by another company. He got a signing bonus. His name appeared in the newspaper. He bought some expensive new suits. His wife remodeled the kitchen.

71.

The boomer had to be tested for cancer. He said if he was okay he would take trivial things less seriously and try to enjoy each day more. He was. He didn't.

72.

To celebrate their anniversary, the boomer and his wife went to Europe. They saw art museums, ate wonderful food, and drank good wine, especially the reds. The boomer thought he could be happy living in Europe because people didn't work as hard and seemed to enjoy life more.

73.

The boomer began to read newspaper stories about hurricanes, mass murders, stock market crashes and wars. While he knew he led a privileged life, he wondered how bad he would feel if it were wiped out.

74.

When he took his son to college, the boomer left him standing in the parking lot in front of the dorm. "Thanks for getting me here," his son said, and walked into the building without looking back.

75.

In the car, the boomer and his wife started to cry. Then they went back to their hotel room and made love more passionately than they had in years.

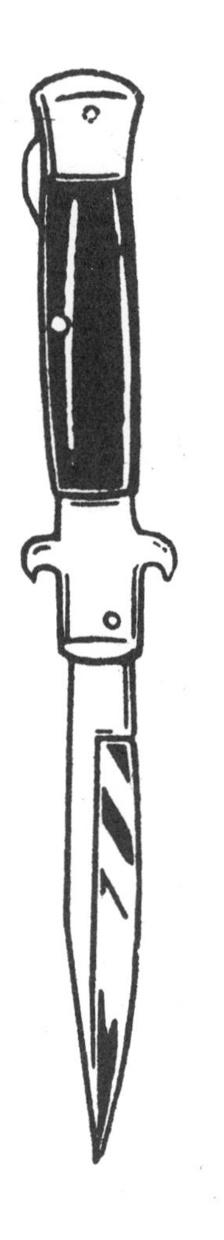

76.

The boomer bought an expensive new home-theater system. It had great bass.

77.

Just before the beginning of his sophomore year, the boomer's son told him he was gay. When the boomer asked if he was sure, his son rolled his eyes.

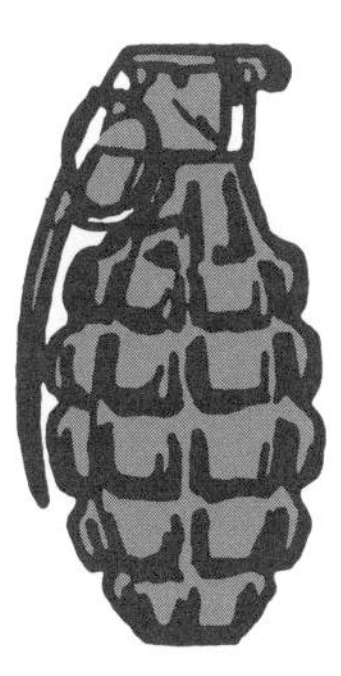

78.

The boomer liked his son's lover. He was from the middle of the country, tall, soft-spoken, and kind. The boomer admired the natural, easy way he showed his affection for his son.

79.

The boomer's wife went back to school to get another degree. She said it made her feel alive to be surrounded by young people. The boomer felt lonely coming home to an empty house. He walked the dog a lot.

80.

When the dog had to be put to sleep, the boomer fell into a depression that neither his third therapist nor his first psychopharmacologist could blunt. When his wife suggested they get a puppy, he said, "No, I want *that* dog."

81.

He couldn't sleep. He arrived and left work at odd hours. He spent lunches browsing pornographic sites and mindlessly trading stocks on the Internet.

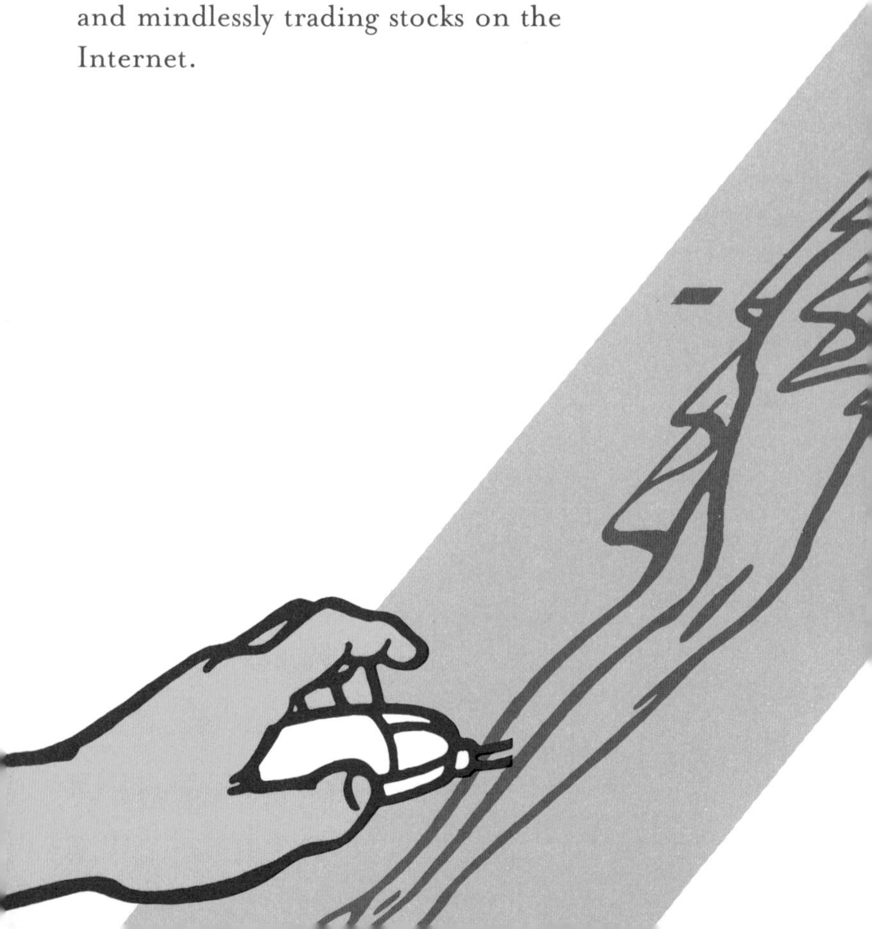

82.

At night he roamed the neighborhood. He drank Scotch. He watched the sun rise.

83.

It was just after dawn when the boomer quietly backed the car out of the driveway.

84.

The Saab cleared the porch and shot through the front of the house in an explosion of shingle and glass. It skidded across the living room until it was finally stopped by the built-in French country bookcases. The Chinese vase toppled from its shelf, landing on the crown of the boomer's head, opening a gash that required fourteen stitches. The vase was unscathed.

85.

The boomer's hospital room looked out on a lower roof populated by some pigeons. He found their jerky, methodical behavior hypnotic. He stared at them until he could identify each one individually.

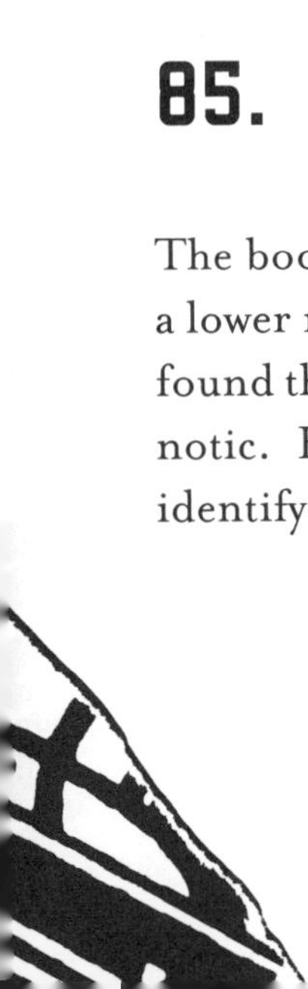

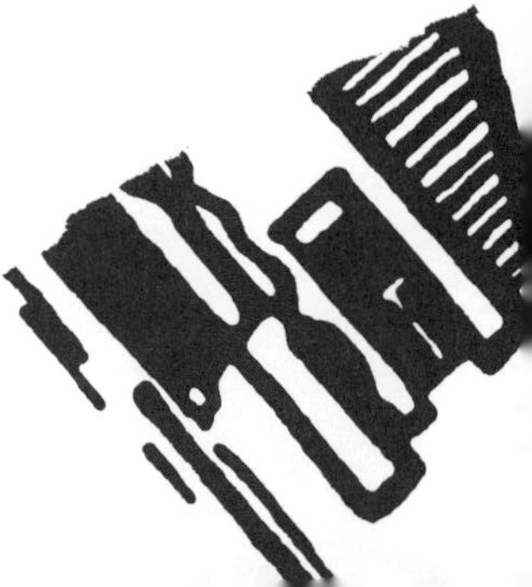

86.

When he awoke, the boomer's wife was at his bedside. "I think you need to go away for a while," she said.

87.

The boomer's son and his lover lived in a small, cheerful condo decorated in white. The boomer slept in the living room. The first morning he woke up at dawn. Outside were birds he had never seen before. He sketched them.

88.

The boomer's son and his son's lover threw a party. They served red, white and blue margaritas. "Which do you prefer?" a woman asked. The boomer tried all three.

89.

The boomer's son and his son's lover adopted a four-year-old boy from another country. The boy did not speak English. The boomer did not speak the boy's language. They communicated by drawing pictures.

90.

The boomer bought the boy a bicycle for his birthday. They went on picnics. They drew.

91.

The boomer moved in with the woman he had met at the party. His son and his son's lover sent them a blender.

92.

They went on a retreat. They meditated. The boomer visualized himself happy. He ate a lot of rice.

93.

Despite all his healthy habits, the boomer developed a serious illness. He received the most advanced treatments and the most aggressive drugs.

94.

The boomer bought a Walkman and fourteen cassettes—*Hot Rocks* by The Rolling Stones, *Bob Dylan's Greatest Hits, Late for the Sky* by Jackson Browne, *Janis Joplin's Greatest Hits, The Best of Eric Clapton, The Best of Steppenwolf, Decade* by Neil Young, *Dark Side of the Moon* by Pink Floyd, *Brothers in Arms* by Dire Straits, *Fleetwood Mac: Greatest Hits, The Best of Marvin Gaye, The Best of Jimi Hendrix, The Essential Beethoven,* and *An Evening with Tchaikovsky.*

95.

He reread *Stranger in a Strange Land, The Lord of the Rings,* and everything by Philip K. Dick.

96.

The boomer wrote a will dividing his estate between his wife

and his son. He left his paintings to his son's lover, who sold the reproduction rights to a greeting card company.

97.

The boomer's ex-wife and her new husband flew in from the southern part of the country, where they had bought a condo that adjoined a golf and tennis center.

98.

The boomer's son and his lover returned from the middle of the country, where they had started an Internet company and bought a house so the boy and his sister could have outdoor space.

99.

The boomer's ex-wife deposited his ashes in the brown Chinese vase. Then she and her new husband, the boomer's son and his lover, the boy and his sister, and the woman he lived with all raised their golf clubs and smashed the vase to bits.

100.

They swept up the shards and ash and buried them in a small, well-tended cemetery with a view of the ocean.

101.

The boomer would have been touched.